For Charlie
A.B.

For Amelia
C.M.

First edition for the United States published 1988 by
Barron's Educational Series, Inc.

First published 1987 by Walker Books Ltd., London, England

Text © Copyright 1987 Antonia Barber
Illustrations © Copyright 1987 Claudio Muñoz

All inquiries should be addressed to:
Barron's Educational Series, Inc.
250 Wireless Boulevard, Hauppauge, NY 11788

Library of Congress Cataloging-in-Publication Data
Barber, Antonia, 1932-
Satchelmouse and the dinosaurs.
Summary: Sarah meets a real dinosaur with the help of
her friend, a mischievous mouse, and his magic trumpet.
[1. Mice–Fiction.   2. Dinosaurs–Fiction]   I. Muñoz,
Claudio, ill.   II. Title.
PZ7.B2323Sap   1988   [E]   87-14513
ISBN 0-8120-5872-0

Printed in Italy
789   9685   987654321

Satchelmouse

and
THE DINOSAURS

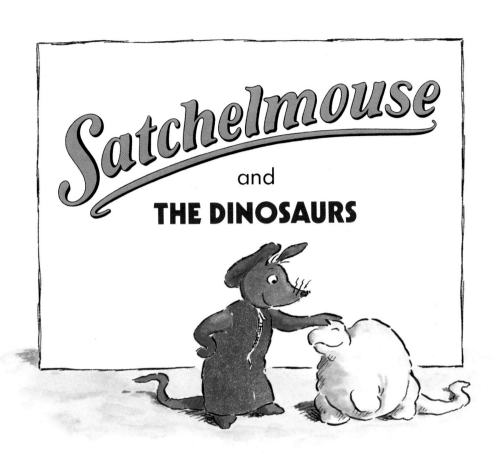

Written by Antonia Barber

Illustrated by Claudio Muñoz

BARRON'S

NEW YORK

The children were learning about the days when dinosaurs roamed the earth.

Mark made tree ferns from cardboard rolls and tissue paper.

Jenny made horsetail plants by cutting straws and fitting them together.

Darren was making a fierce tyrannosaurus out of papier mâché.

Sarah was trying to make a diplodocus with modeling clay, but it kept going wrong.

Sarah had a special friend, a tall brown mouse named Satchelmouse.

Inside his red jacket was a pencil case full of useful things.

The pencil sharpener was a golden trumpet and only Sarah knew that it had magic powers.

When Satchelmouse saw the diplodocus, he wrinkled up his long nose.

"It's too small," he said.

"It's a baby one," said Sarah quickly. "They must have had babies."

"The neck should be longer."

"Maybe their necks get longer when they are older," said Sarah hopefully.

Satchelmouse looked doubtful. "One of its legs is too short," he said.

Sarah gave up. "How can I make a diplodocus when I've never even seen one?" she asked crossly.

"Never seen a diplodocus?" Satchelmouse laughed. "I can soon fix that."

He blew his golden trumpet and the magic began.

Sarah found herself in a strange forest.

Tall tree ferns reached high overhead and giant horsetails grew all around.

There was a roaring noise in the distance which she did not like at all.

Something was coming through the forest toward them.

Sarah picked up Satchelmouse. "Quick! We must hide!" she said.

They dived into a big bunch of horsetails
and peered out cautiously.

It was a baby diplodocus and
it was limping.

It looked around for somewhere to hide
and saw Sarah's startled face.

"Help me!" it said. "The tyrannosaurus
is chasing me."

The roaring noise was growing louder.

"I can't run very fast," explained the little diplodocus sadly. "One of my legs is too short."

Sarah still had some modeling clay in her hand. "I could make your leg longer if you like," she offered.

The diplodocus was very grateful. It balanced on three feet and held out the other one for Sarah to mend.

When she had finished, it jumped around with little cries of joy.

Sarah was afraid that the tyrannosaurus would hear it.

"Haven't you got a mother to look after you?" she asked.

"I've lost her." The little diplodocus looked sad again. "If only my neck were longer I could look over the treetops and find her."

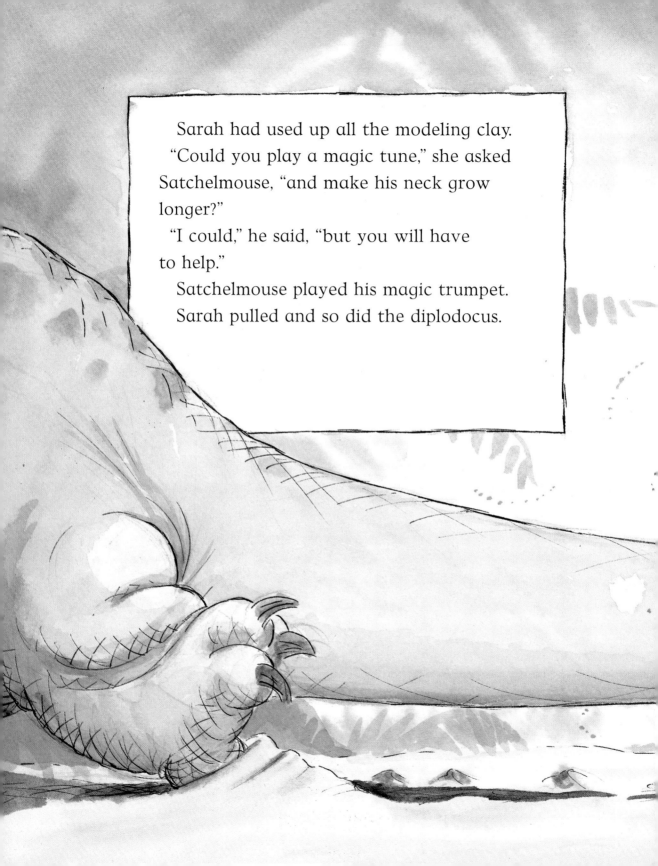

Sarah had used up all the modeling clay.
"Could you play a magic tune," she asked
Satchelmouse, "and make his neck grow
longer?"

"I could," he said, "but you will have
to help."

Satchelmouse played his magic trumpet.
Sarah pulled and so did the diplodocus.

Soon its neck was so long that it could look over the tops of the tree ferns.

"Oh, thank you!" said the little diplodocus. "I can see my mother now!" And it went bounding off toward her through the forest.

The roaring noise was very close.

"Quick! Blow your trumpet!" said Sarah to Satchelmouse. "I want to go back to school."

But the tyrannosaurus had already found them.

Sarah saw its big white teeth gleaming as it opened its mouth to gobble her up.

"Help!" she shouted. But Satchelmouse was hiding under some ferns.

Sarah thought she heard the faintest trumpet squeak.

Suddenly all the big white teeth vanished. The fierce tyrannosaurus did not have a single tooth in its head!

Sarah found that she was back in the classroom.

Satchelmouse was under her chair.

As Sarah picked him up she heard Darren say, "Stupid tyrannosaurus! His teeth have fallen out."

Mrs. James liked the diplodocus. "It looks very real," she said.

Sarah laughed and picked up a big lump of modeling clay.

"I'm going to make a mother for him now," she said.